Double
Twist

KINGFISHER
Kingfisher Publications plc
New Penderel House
283-288 High Holborn
London WC1V 7HZ
www.kingfisherpub.com

First published in 2007
2 4 6 8 10 9 7 5 3 1

ISBN: 978 07534 1357 9

Printed in India
1TR/0107/THOM/SCHOY/80STORA/C

Double Twist

DONNA KING

KINGFISHER

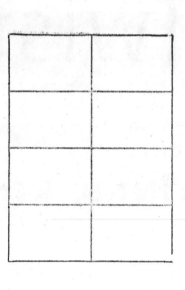

CHAPTER 1

"Most kids spend their summer holiday sunning themselves on a beach in Spain," Jack Lee muttered to his younger sister, Laura. "So how come you're standing here shivering at the side of an ice rink?"

"Because I'm a child star!" Laura grinned. "A genius on ice!"

Jack zipped his jacket to his chin. "Says who?"

"Says Mum." Laura waited impatiently for the public session to end so she could skate onto the ice for her private coaching with Vera Mozer, while Jack went to play five-a-side soccer. Their mum was due to pick her up later. "Where's Patrick?" Jack wondered out loud.

"Don't worry, he'll be here." Laura watched the little kids on the ice. They whizzed around the rink like demons, in and out of the grown-ups, who wobbled and crashed down like skittles. One or two older kids tried out turns and spins, taking the whole thing more seriously. "Patrick's never late," she added.

Jack glanced back at the entrance, spied Laura's tall, serious ice-dance partner and yelled out his name. "Hey, Patrick, over here!" Now he could scoot.

Patrick joined them. He was wearing a thick padded jacket and a scarf wound high around his neck. "Hey," he said quietly.

"Where are your folks?" Jack asked.

"Mum and Dad? They dropped me off, then went to the bank. They'll be back in a few minutes."

"So is it okay if I shoot off?"

Laura and Patrick nodded. Laura was grinning at the sight of another grown-up biting the dust. The middle-aged woman squealed as she went down, smack on her bum. "Oops!"

"Don't laugh!" Patrick bit his lip and looked away.

"She's down! Now she's up and brushing ice off herself . . . oops, she's down again!" Eventually the poor woman made it to the edge of the rink and clung onto the rail. "Why isn't she at home watching telly and knitting woolly hats for her grandkids?"

"Laura!" Patrick shook his head, glad when the siren sounded for people to clear the ice. At least now Laura wouldn't be able to make fun of old ladies.

"Lighten up!" Laura giggled, waving to a couple of kids she knew from school as they came off the ice. "Hey, Georgina, hey, Abi!"

"Are you here to train?" Abi asked as she bent down to take off her skates.

"Yep. Why?"

"Just wondered if you wanted to join us in the café."

"Thanks, I'd love to, but we've got a big competition coming up. Got to keep practising those twizzles!"

"Poor you!" Abi grinned. "Where are you jetting off to this time?"

"Montreal, in just under a month."

"Canada?" Abi's jaw dropped. "Wow!"

"Junior Grand Prix," Patrick chipped in. "We're in the running for a medal if we work hard."

Georgina tugged at her mate's arm. "C'mon, I'm starving!"

"Well, good luck!" Abi said to Laura and Patrick. "Wow, Canada . . . cool!"

"Laura, you need more leg and foot extension in that third section!" Vera's eagle eye didn't miss a thing. "Patrick, you were too close to the boards on the synchronised leg swing!"

"Sorry!" Laura told her partner under her breath. They'd been working non-stop for an hour and her concentration was beginning to slip. "This compulsory section isn't my thing."

"We've still got to get it right," he insisted. "Let's do it one more time."

They took up position in the centre of the empty rink. Their coach watched from the barrier. "I'm asking a lot of you with this paso doble," she called. "You have to dance exactly to the beat and keep the Latin spirit going, while at the same time getting those twizzles right and leading smoothly into the lift. Okay, try again!"

Laura heard the music start. She noticed Patrick's mum and dad behind Vera, and then her own mum joining them. With this audience, she knew she'd better get her act together. *Leg and foot extension!* she reminded herself. *Synchronised leg swings!*

Together, she and Patrick sprang into action. This rhythm was tricky – it was fast and dramatic, and if you missed a beat the whole thing went wrong.

"Laura, your foot was loose on that

diagonal sequence; Patrick, you over-rotated on the landing of that throw double loop!"

Once more Vera picked up on every tiny error and bellowed out across the ice. It was what you'd expect from a woman who had been an Olympic ice-dance gold-medal-winner herself. She never let you get away with a single thing.

Laura linked hands with Patrick for another lift, using their speed to get her off the ground, spreading her arms wide as he hoisted her into the air. She saw the overhead lights turn to a blur as Patrick spun her, remembered her leg and foot extension, felt herself lowered and her blades make contact with the ice.

"Good!" Vera called.

Laura made eye contact with her partner and grinned. *Definite praise from the great ex-champion – wow!*

They got their leg lines sorted out on the next turn sequence, then made their grand finish, arms flung wide, backs arched like Spanish bullfighters.

"Whoa!" Laura gasped. She relaxed her position and gave her mum a quick wave. "Patrick, I think we just did the whole thing without a fault!"

He nodded happily, his grey eyes gleaming, waving at his own mum and dad as he and Laura skated towards Vera to hear her verdict.

Their coach gave them a hard look from underneath her fur hat, standing with her hands in her pockets, clicking her tongue against the roof of her mouth. "Not bad," she said slowly in her thick accent. "But not the best. Now go, do it all again!"

CHAPTER 2

"Read me a story!" Laura's little sister, Imogen, plonked down on the sofa beside her and thrust a big picture book under her face.

"Not now, Immy, I'm tired." And bruised and battered from a fall she'd taken at the end of their latest coaching session. She and Patrick hadn't timed a lift properly and she'd crashed to the ice doing what felt like 30 miles per hour. Now all she needed was a hot chocolate and some TV.

"Puh-lease!" Immy begged, her five-year-old face screwing up into a soulful expression. "It's about a giant with a bad headache – look!"

"I've got a bad headache all of my own!"

Laura sighed, giving in and taking the book. "'George the Giant woke up one morning with a giant headache,'" she read, while Immy stared at the pictures. "'He got out of his giant bed and put on his giant slippers . . .'"

". . . And took a giant headache pill and lived happily ever after!" Laura's younger brother, James, gabbled, his mouth full of breakfast cereal. He came and snatched the book. "Cut the giant stuff, Laura, I'm trying to watch telly!"

Immy gave a high wail and ran off to complain to their dad. Jack snatched the remote and flicked through the channels until he found football.

"Happy families!" Laura grinned, stretching out on the sofa and testing out her bruises. In her head she was going through the routine that she and Patrick would have to practise tomorrow – a smooth and silky salsa changing to a slower rumba, then back to the salsa. With luck, her bruises wouldn't hurt too much. "Ouch!" she groaned as she pressed a tender spot.

Then Immy came back to practise trampoline on the sofa and Jimmy had a fight with Jack over the remote.

If we fall on that curved lift, we have to get up and skate on! Laura reminded herself, getting up from the sofa and silently going through the motions of the routine in a kind of crazy mime. *And we don't skate through the music, we keep to the beat!*

"Where's my giant book?!" Immy clamoured, bouncing up and down.

"Give me that remote!" Jimmy yelled.

"Goal!" Jack roared, punching the air with his fist.

Tony Lee walked in on the chaos. "Good God!" he muttered. One daughter was wrecking the sofa. The other had her legs in the air like a lunatic. The two boys were threatening to maim each other for life. "It's a miracle that anyone survives in this house!"

And he turned around and disappeared into his study.

"Suppertime!" the kids' mum yelled from the kitchen. "Immy, Jimmy, Laura, Jack – come and eat!"

It was only in bed that night that Laura finally wound down. She'd been on the move since six, with her early-morning coaching session followed by shopping with Abi, followed by taking Immy to the park, followed by her teatime training session with Vera. But that was a normal summer day for Laura – sprinting from this to that, dreaming of Montreal.

We can win a medal! she told herself, snuggled under her duvet, staring up at the dark ceiling. *Okay, so we have to beat the Americans and the Italians, not to mention the Canadian and Russian couples, but our routines are great on content, thanks to Vera, and it's up to Patrick and me to get our technique perfect during the next two weeks!*

Though Laura's body was finally resting, her mind would not switch off. *I can't believe I'm going to Canada! Of course, I've seen it on TV – snow on the Rocky Mountains and everything. And I've been lots of places already – Bulgaria and the Czech Republic, plus London lots of times, which is amazing. But I've never been to Montreal!*

Laura heard her dad come upstairs, switching off lights as he went. She heard the bedroom door open and close.

Go to sleep! she told herself, but she couldn't. *Maybe we'll get a medal!* she thought, her head in a whirl. *We were fourth in Andorra, just behind the Italians. Our three programmes are better this time. If we skate really well, I'm sure we can get into the medals! And if we don't, so what?*

For a while Laura lay still, trying to picture the event in Montreal. She saw pairs of skaters in brilliant costumes – some in bright scarlet and gold, some in pale blue, others in white and silver, turquoise and purple. She saw the bright lights shining down on the pure white ice, heard the music begin for her and Patrick . . .

If we don't win, we'll still have a really cool time, she told herself. *We'll skate as well as we can and have fun. I mean, what could be better than arriving in Canada with Vera, putting in our last training sessions, then getting out there in front of all those people?*

The question floated in the darkness.

Nothing! she answered herself, finally turning over and getting ready to sleep. *There is nothing in this whole world better than being on the ice with Patrick, skating our dream!*

"Try the step sequence again," Vera ordered. "Patrick, your right foot is still weaker than your left. Laura, you need more body contact with Patrick!"

Salsa! Snaky hips, back bends and arm flicks. Laura danced to the music, working out a tricky combination of steps across the ice. She was tired this morning because of not sleeping well the night before, but she still threw herself into the training session with every ounce of energy she had. *If you're going to do something, do it 100 percent – da-da-duh-dah!*

"Okay, come over here," Vera called when they'd completed the sequence.

Laura let go of Patrick's arm and skated smoothly to the barrier.

"You were late for the second twizzle," Patrick muttered as he followed.

Laura frowned. She was sure she hadn't been late. "No, you were early," she mumbled back.

Just lately, she and Patrick had been having these little squabbles. He was always finding fault and she was too feisty to let it pass.

"You were late," he insisted, skating to a halt in front of Vera.

"Patrick, don't skate ahead of the music," their coach told him. "And try to look as if you're having fun!"

He looked down at the ice, breathing hard and trying to catch his breath. Laura said nothing, but she thought, *I told you so!*

"Listen," Vera went on, her breath clouding the cold air. "The salsa section has to be fun to do and fun to watch, otherwise forget it. Then, when you slow down for the rumba section, when the trumpet comes in, you must look at each other and skate as if you are in love!"

Laura watched Patrick's face. He blushed and coughed, as if clearing his throat. *Oh no, the 'love' word!*

"Patrick, you hear what I'm saying?"

"Yeah," he muttered, looking as if he wanted the ice to melt and swallow him.

Lighten up! Laura tried not to giggle. *It's not as if Vera's actually telling you to fancy me in real life!* The idea made the embarrassed laugh rise to the surface. *I mean, we've been skating together since we were eight!*

"Don't be shy," the coach continued in her deep, Russian voice. "Enjoy!"

"Shall we do it again?" Laura was revving up, ready to go, tightening her ponytail and hooking back strands of dark hair.

Vera looked hard at Patrick. "No, we'll take a break. Come, sit!"

They came off the ice and sat on a bench, listening to their coach's advice. "Laura, you look tired today. You need to get more sleep. Patrick, you are skating with the weight of the world on your shoulders. Go away from here and have fun."

"I'd rather practise some more," he said, sitting hunched forward, knees wide apart, hands clasped. His eyes were worried. "We've got less than four weeks to go."

"Is something the matter?" Vera picked up a problem and as usual got straight to the point. "Tell me. Is it your father?"

Patrick took a deep breath. "He's putting pressure on me at home," he admitted. "I get it in the neck all the time – practise more, eat properly, build up your strength, blah-blah!"

"Wow!" Laura thought of her own dad – so laidback he almost fell over. If anything, it was her mum who pushed Laura on to succeed.

"Your father is right," Vera insisted. "All these things are important. But you must also have a life outside skating. Go to a movie, chill out."

Laura's eyes widened in surprise. Was she hearing right?

"I mean it," Vera said, looking at her watch and discovering that it was time for the ice rink to open up to the public. She took off her big fur hat to reveal a helmet of flattened blonde hair. "So, we all want a medal in Montreal more than we've ever wanted anything in our whole lives. We want to go there and show that we are the best, right?"

Laura and Patrick nodded, aware that the first skaters were arriving on the ice. Laura saw Abi and waved.

"We are good," Vera insisted. "We have

worked hard all summer. We have a fabulous programme for you to skate."

Level-four lifts, serpentine steps, combination spins . . . Laura knew for sure that these things would impress the Montreal judges.

"But Patrick, the fun is not there for you. And too much pressure means you make mistakes."

"So can somebody tell me how you make yourself relax?" he muttered, seeing his mum and dad in the distance and standing up from the bench.

"Just come to my house for an afternoon!" Laura joked. "My brother Jack can give you lessons in vegging out, no problem!"

Patrick didn't smile. Instead, he took off his boots and went to join his parents.

Hmm," Vera said, shaking her head. "That boy!"

"I know," Laura agreed. *Way too serious, way too uptight.*

She looked at the rink, now crowded with people having fun. Okay, so some of them could hardly skate a step, but they were laughing as they fell over, and friends were hauling them back onto their feet.

"See you tomorrow morning, early," Vera told her, heading for the exit.

"See you," Laura replied. She watched a tiny kid zooming over the ice followed by his nervous dad. Then a couple of cool girls about the same age as her, looking good and knowing it in their bright, slinky tops, were showing off in front of the boys.

A group of noisy kids skated behind the two girls round the ice, for one full circuit, until one boy broke away and decided to do some showing-off of his own. He put on a burst of speed to find a clear patch of ice then started a spin – slow at first, then, tucking his arms across his chest, getting faster and faster.

Wow! Laura thought. *He can skate!*

The boy, who was maybe thirteen or fourteen, came out of the spin and struck out across the path of the two girls, putting in a couple of turns. He was laughing and calling to his mates, who jostled and kidded.

"Hey, Scott!" one called. "Show Alexa and Hannah that hip-hop thing!"

He laughed and began to swing his arms, picking up a rhythm with his feet.

"Show off!" the first girl said, flicking her hair back.

"Scott Yorke, you're so-o-o not clever!" the second scoffed.

I don't know about that, Laura thought, looking with a well-trained eye. *I'd say he was pretty neat. Good rhythm, smooth steps.*

The boy shrugged, put in another turn then skated off into the crowd.

Laura watched him disappear – a tall, sporty kid with short, black hair, wearing a cool T-shirt and jeans.

"You can say one thing for sure," Laura sighed, thinking of Patrick and turning away from the ice. "That hip-hop kid knows how to have fun!"

CHAPTER 3

"Everything okay?" Laura's mum asked early the following morning.

Helen Lee got up at five every day except Sunday, spring, summer, autumn and winter, to make sure Laura got to the ice rink on time. Somehow she managed to be bright and cheerful, even at that time of day.

"Yeah, ready," Laura said, grabbing a last mouthful of toast and a quick gulp of orange juice.

"Tony, make sure Immy gets up in time for her doctor's appointment at nine!" Helen called upstairs. "She's having her ears checked, remember. And kick Jack out at seven for his paper round. Oh, and Jimmy is going to Adam's house this morning. His mum says to drop him off at nine-thirty . . . "

There was no reply from the bedroom, but Laura knew her dad would somehow manage to get everything sorted. She got into the car, ready to doze on the way to the rink.

"How are you feeling?" her mum asked as they drove through the deserted streets.

"Good."

"Not too nervous about the Grand Prix?"

"Nope." *Z-z-z-z-z.*

"How about Patrick?"

"Patrick's Patrick – y'know."

"How does Vera think you'll do in Montreal?"

"Depends." *Z-z-z-z.* "Mum, no more questions – let me sleep, okay?"

Laura dozed off and before she knew it they were pulling up in the empty car park where there was only last night's litter blowing in the morning breeze and a couple of pigeons pecking at someone's abandoned take-away. *Charming!*

"Are you staying or going?" she asked her mum.

"Staying." Helen handed Laura her sports bag. "I'm not working until midday today. It'll be good to see how you're getting on."

"Mum, we're doing great!" Laura protested. Today she felt she could do without the extra pressure of being watched. "I hope you're not turning into Patrick's mum and dad!"

Helen laughed. "'Tell me, Vera, is Laura working as hard as she should?'" She copied Mrs Cole's prim voice.

"Yeah, whatever!" Smiling, Laura swung in through the main door and went to get changed, brushing her hair back from her face and putting on tights and a red practice top and skirt. She carried her skates under her arm as she headed for the rink.

By now Patrick was there, for once minus his mum and dad. Vera too was waiting.

"Hey," Laura said, quickly putting on her

skates. "Are you okay?" she checked with him.

He nodded. "I'm kind of tired," he admitted. "Not enough sleep last night."

"Me neither." Laura saw his pinched face and decided that he was still stressed out.

Vera stepped in. "Today I think we should concentrate on our rumba section for the original programme. Okay, go ahead."

"Oops, this is the bit I'm worried about," Laura admitted. It was the so-called romantic section where she and Patrick had to be lovey-dovey.

"*You're* worried!" he sighed. "Dad's already been on my case today – I don't skate fast enough, I'm not throwing high enough, blah blah, yackety-yack!

She grinned. "Yeah, he's like Vera – nothing's ever good enough!" Across the rink, their coach was in conversation with her mum.

"Better put on a good performance, then," she said as she and Patrick took to the ice.

Take the centre of the rink, hold Patrick's hand, wait for the music to start. Look totally confident!

The opening notes for the rumba floated across the ice. The two women came close to the barrier to watch every move.

"Okay?" Laura muttered under her breath.

Patrick nodded, his face tense and pale.

Hold hands and glide smoothly forward, picking up speed. Skate as close to the barrier as we can, swoop around in a wide arc, prepare for the first lift!

Their blades sliced through the smooth, glistening surface of the ice, sending up cold white powder. They moved fast and Patrick prepared to take Laura's weight on his right shoulder. She felt herself rise high in the air, flung her arms wide, arched her back and flew.

Behind the barrier, Helen Lee applauded the lift while Vera made notes.

Land smoothly, without a jolt, keep my balance, wait for Patrick to catch up . . . We did it!

The nerve-wracking lift was over. Laura could relax.

The music played on; a trumpet sounded, slow and soulful. But Patrick was half a beat off-tempo, skating slightly behind her.

He's tired, Laura reminded herself, waiting for him to catch up before they sped across the centre of the rink and went into their synchronised double twist. Then a lift.

No problem, we can do this! she thought. *We've done it a thousand times before!*

Once more Patrick had to use their speed to lift her. He threw her into the air, spinning her high, speeding close to the barrier where their stern coach stood. So close, in fact, that the back edge of his left skate clicked against the metal board.

Laura heard the click as she landed. She glanced round to see her partner struggling to keep his balance. His arms flew wide, he leaned backwards, his skates churning up the ice. Then he lost it and toppled against the barrier, landing in a heap as the high trumpet notes played on.

He's down! He's not getting up to re-start. He's not even moving! Quickly Laura broke out of the routine and skated back towards Patrick. "What happened?" she cried, bending over him.

"It's my knee!" he groaned, his face white, his mouth twisted with pain.

"Keep still, don't move!" Vera yelled as she strode onto the ice. She checked the knee then shook her head. "You dislocated the joint," she told him. "We need to get you straight to the hospital."

Laura crouched on the ice beside him. "Don't worry, you'll be okay," she whispered, as if by saying it she could hang onto their dream.

"What about Montreal?" Patrick gasped, the pain still showing in his face.

Yeah, the World Junior Championship – mine and Patrick's big chance! Laura looked anxiously at their coach.

Vera sighed and gave it to them straight.

"You can forget it," she said firmly. "I can tell you now, Patrick – no way is this leg injury going to heal in time!

Helen Lee called Mr and Mrs Cole, who arrived at the rink at the same time as the ambulance that was taking their son to casualty. They met up in the empty car park, where Laura and Vera watched the paramedics carry the stretcher away.

Mrs Cole rushed straight to her son, while Mr Cole approached Vera. "How bad is it?" he asked.

"Pretty bad." Vera hadn't held back before and she didn't now. "They'll have to X-ray the knee and push the joint back into position."

"How long for it to get better?"

Vera shrugged. "We don't know how much damage has been done to the ligaments. Also, the bone might be cracked."

Laura shivered as the ambulance door

closed behind Patrick. She re-lived the moment when the accident had happened, wishing with all her might that life was something you could rewind to a certain point, before things went wrong, and then start over.

Mr Cole shook his head in disbelief then glanced at Laura. "Whose fault was this?"

"Nobody's fault, Mr Cole," Vera said firmly. "Patrick had an unlucky accident, that's all. It happens in ice skating."

"It couldn't come at a worse time," Patrick's father fretted as his wife came to talk to him.

"We have to follow the ambulance," she told her husband.

"I'll come too," Vera decided, quickly saying goodbye to Laura and Helen. "I'm so sorry this has happened!" she told them quietly, for once dropping her stern front and letting her emotions show. "I had high hopes for Montreal and my little Laura!"

For the first time Laura felt tears coming.

She sniffed them back. "Me too," she murmured. It was weird what happened when a dream was shattered – you were left feeling shocked and empty, until someone told you they were sorry. Then the tears put in an appearance.

"Come on," her mum said, taking her by the arm. "Let's get you home."

"There'll be other chances," Tony Lee told his daughter.

Laura had moped around the house all day, getting news from the hospital before lunch that Patrick's kneecap was actually broken, as well as pushed out of place.

"That's that," her mum had said before she left for work. "There's no chance of him being fit to skate for at least three months."

That's that. Finish. End of story. Laura had drifted from room to room, ignoring Immy's demands to play a game of Twister. The afternoon had passed by in a dull daze.

But now her dad had sat her down and started giving her advice.

"Listen, honey, I know this must hurt. You'd built your hopes up so high about getting to Canada and winning a medal. But life doesn't always work out the way we want it to."

Why doesn't it? Laura thought. *Patrick and I worked all year for this. It's just not fair!*

"Laura, are you listening?"

She nodded. "Yeah, Dad. Sorry."

"Like I say, there'll be another chance. Just give Patrick's leg time to heal, then start again."

"It'll be too late," she sighed. "We'll slip way down the rankings. No one will even look at us next time we enter a competition."

"Of course they will. You two are very talented skaters. There's no way that's going to change."

At last Laura managed to look up. It wasn't her father's usual style to hand out the praise. He said it was in case she got too big-headed. "Do you mean that, Dad? Do you really think we're talented?"

He grinned. "Big time!"

"Wow! Suddenly I feel loads better."

"Good." Her dad patted her on the knee then left to find out why Immy was wailing and knee-deep in feathers up in her bedroom. "What happened to your duvet?" Laura heard him say.

Okay, she said to herself. *Enough feeling sorry for yourself! What about poor Patrick? Note to self — better visit him tomorrow.*

"Hey, tough news about Patrick, kiddo!" Jack said, poking his head around the lounge door. "But look at it this way — no more early-morning workouts!"

Laura managed to smile.

A few minutes later, Jimmy came in to flick on the TV. He glanced at Laura. "Jack said you were blubbing about not going to Canada!"

"I'm so-o-o not!" she protested, getting up and whacking him with a cushion.

". . . Anyway, who says I'm not going?"

"You can't go if you don't have a partner, dummy!"

Laura frowned. Suddenly she wanted to fight back. "Who says I don't have a partner?"

Jimmy turned up the volume. "Patrick broke his leg, dumbo!"

"So . . . maybe I can find a new one."

"Da-dah-di-dah!" Jimmy blocked his ears.

Giving up, Laura flounced out of the room. Okay, so she knew better than to expect sympathy from Jimmy. But hey, what had she just said? *Maybe I can find a new partner.*

Laura stopped in the hallway and thought about it. *A new partner. Where? How?*

Don't be stupid – there's only a month to go before Montreal. How can you find someone new?

"There must be a kid who can skate around here somewhere," she murmured.

Go on then. Go ahead – perform a miracle and find him!

Laura shook her head to get rid of the

doubting voice. "You think I can't do miracles? Just watch me!"

So, you find the boy wonder, the new, undiscovered skating genius. But how is he going to learn the routines in time?

She shook her head again. "Shut up!" she told the nuisance voice. "You know me. If I set my heart on doing something, I do it!"

"Talking to yourself?" Jack teased as he flew downstairs three at a time and vanished into the lounge.

"What are you up to, Laura?" her dad asked, standing with a feather-covered Immy at the top of the stairs.

She looked up at him with a determined light in her eye, taking her jacket off the hook. "I'm going to the ice rink," she told him without stopping to explain. "Don't worry, I'll be back home by seven!"

CHAPTER 4

On Friday night the ice rink was always humming. The skaters were mostly kids. There were hardly any grown-ups. Laura queued for admission, impatient to get through the turnstile onto the ice.

"I fancy a Big Mac after we finish here," the boy in front said to his mates, glancing back at Laura. "Hey, aren't you . . . ?"

"Yeah, she's the girl who does the fancy routines before they let the rabble in," his friend said.

Laura shrugged and tried to turn away, but now everyone started to recognise her.

"What are you training for? Are you really famous?" one girl in the queue wanted to know.

"How do you do all those spin things?" another asked.

At last it was Laura's turn to pay. Quickly she handed over her money and slipped through the turnstile, heading straight for the ice, where all her awkwardness fell away. After all, while she was skating, no one could get at her.

For a while she glided across the smooth surface, swerving between other skaters, soaking up the sights and sounds, just chilling. This felt good, she decided – being one of the crowd, feeling happy, no worries.

But then she remembered why she had come. *You're here to talent scout,* she reminded herself. *There's got to be someone here who's a cool skater. Okay, so maybe he won't be trained, maybe he'll just be here to have fun. But he'll have real skill!*

As Laura began to look around, her hopes of working a miracle were soon dented. For a start, as usual there were more people falling over than skating smoothly. Some would take a few faltering steps, then lose their balance; others would wobble on for longer, then crash against the barrier, unable to stop. Their friends would haul them up from the ice and drag them on.

Huh! Laura frowned and skated, threading her way between the laughing knots of kids. *Where's that kid I saw here before? The one they called Scott? I reckoned he'd be here on a Friday night.*

But she couldn't pick out his dark hair and cool T-shirt, and she had to concentrate hard to steer clear of the tumbling, toppling bodies that littered the ice. After half an hour, she was ready to give up and head for home.

"Watch out!" A cry came from behind her and a figure hurtled towards her.

Laura swerved to avoid a crash. The boy was out of control, on a collision course with the barrier.

"Ouch!" Laura grimaced as she anticipated the sudden stop.

"Oof!" The boy hit the barrier and knocked the breath from his body. Soon he was surrounded by half a dozen mates who picked him up and dusted him down.

"Stand up, Will! . . . Man, you hit that wall hard! . . . Can you breathe? . . . Will, talk to us!"

"Okay, cool – I'm good!" At last the boy got back on his feet and the crowd surrounding him melted away, leaving only the very person Laura had been looking for.

Scott's here! Wow, this is my lucky night!

"Do you want to stay or leave?" Scott checked with his mate, helping him across the ice.

Laura started up after them, hanging back a little, wondering what to do next.

"No, I'll stay. I'm good," Will insisted, brushing off the whole thing. "Just a little technical problem with my brakes, that's all!"

Scott laughed. "You've got to learn how to turn, man!"

"So show me."

Laura watched as Scott skated ahead.

"This is how you do it. I can't tell you exactly – I guess it's to do with leaning on one side of the blades and using the weight of your body. I never really thought about it."

No, but you can do it without thinking! Watching closely, Laura was sure that Scott was a natural skater. He had great flow and balance, almost as if he'd been born with ice skates on his feet. She allowed her hopes to rise again.

"So how do you stop?" novice Will asked.

Scott showed him and made him do it. "It's a bit like skiing," he explained. "Did you ever go skiing?"

Will shook his head. "I play anything with a ball," he confessed, "but put me on a slippery surface and I'm dead! C'mon, I'm out of here. Let's go and get a cold drink."

Okay, this is it! Laura decided. *It's now or never!* She skated up to the two boys. "This might sound weird," she began . . .

"No way!" was the first thing Scott said.

"You've got to be kidding!" Will laughed.

"I mean it – I need a new partner!" Laura stood on the crowded ice, trying to make Scott believe she was serious.

"I don't do ice dance!" Scott told her. "Okay, so these are figure skates – I borrowed them from my dad. He used to do a few twirls on the ice. But not me. Now, if you'd said ice hockey, I might be interested. I played a lot last winter."

"Ice dance!" Will echoed mockingly.

"Listen, my partner just got injured. Scott, I saw you skate hip hop on the ice the other day and I've been watching you again today – you're a good skater!"

Scott grimaced then shrugged. "Yeah, I

like it. But ice *dance*?"

"What's wrong with that?" Laura wanted to know. "You'd better not diss it. You've got to be tough to get through all the training – especially the lifting."

"You don't get it," Will interrupted, speaking up for his mate. "Scott's thing is soccer. He plays with me in United's junior squad."

"Yeah, that's cool," Laura went on. "My big brother is soccer-crazy too." She thought she'd spotted a glimmer of interest in Scott's eyes, in spite of what Will had said. "But this would only be four weeks out of your life. Y'know, like on TV – where they take someone who works in an office and turn them into an opera singer or something and then they fool the professional judges!"

"Four weeks?" he repeated. "Then what?"

"Then we fly to Canada. International Junior Grand Prix in Montreal. Then back to school and you can play all the soccer you want for the rest of your life!"

Now there was a definite light shining through the questions and doubts. "Montreal?" Scott murmured.

"Man, you're not taking this stuff seriously?" Will scoffed, backing off and shaking his head. "You're Mister Cool. You don't do ice dance!"

"No way!" Scott toughed it out in front of Will. "I'm not even thinking of saying yes."

"Okay, cool," Will grunted, wobbling off on his skates to join the rest of the gang.

Scott narrowed his eyes and looked back at Laura. "Canada?" he checked again.

She nodded. Now that she had Scott on his own, she felt she might be able to persuade him. "If you're good enough. And if your parents agree." Laura felt that Scott's dad's ice-skating history might help here. She'd checked Scott's skates closely and saw they were pretty well made, which meant that his dad had been a serious skater in his time.

"My dad will be cool," he told her, confirming her gut feeling. "My mum's not around any more."

"Okay, so it comes down to whether you'll be good enough."

Scott thought a while longer. "Do I have to wear tights?"

She grinned. "No."

"Sequins?"

"Not if you don't want to." *Yes, he's weakening!* she thought.

"No sequins." Scott laid it on the line. "Who'll teach me? . . . If I say I'll do it!"

Laura took a deep breath. "Me to start with. Then there's my coach, Vera Mozer. She was an Olympic champion in the 1980s. She's the best."

Scott nodded, thinking it through. "I've seen you training with her," he confessed. "You're pretty good."

"Thanks. So?" She still held her breath, waiting for the answer. *This could make all the difference!*

"Okay, I'll do it!" Scott said. "When do we start?"

Saturday morning, early. Only Laura and Scott were on the ice. Inside the empty rink, the music echoed.

"It's called a paso doble," Laura told Scott. "Listen to the beat. It's a bit tricky, but once you've got it in your head, you can take two steps and kick with your right leg, like this."

Scott yawned. "It's too early," he moaned. "I should be at home in bed!"

"Watch!" Laura skated the steps again. "Now you do it."

Her new partner shrugged and copied her perfectly.

"Cool." Laura was surprised by how easily he did it. "Now add a back swing and a ninety-degree turn on your left leg, like this."

Scott watched carefully. "What are you doing with your arms?"

"Pretending to be a bull fighter waving his cape. You have to get into the spirit of the dance."

"Man!" Scott groaned, reluctantly copying Laura's arm movements.

"Quit whingeing. After the quarter turn, we link arms and take five steps on the diagonal, then you have to lift me."

"Hey, slow down!" Scott struggled to follow. "This lift — do we have to try it right now?"

Laura shook her head. "Do I look stupid? No way would I trust you with the lifts until we've worked them out in the gym."

"Who said anything about a gym?"

"I did. Tonight, after your soccer match."

Scott made the face of a small kid who's been kept back after school. "Do I have to?"

Laura laughed and nodded. "No gain without pain," she told him. "Think Canada. Think Montreal. Now c'mon, try this diagonal sequence again!"

★ ★ ★

"I hate hospitals," Patrick admitted when Laura visited him that afternoon.

He was in a bed with a cage over his broken leg, propped up on pillows and looking pale and bored.

She'd brought grapes, which they sat and ate together.

"How have your mum and dad taken it?" Laura asked, fidgeting on her seat.

Patrick wrinkled his nose, looking upset. "You know . . ."

"Yeah, I can guess." His parents were probably giving him a hard time without meaning to. They wouldn't be able to hide their disappointment over him missing Montreal. "Does the leg hurt?"

He nodded. "Why did this have to happen?"

"I know, it sucks." Laura wondered about mentioning Scott then decided against it. After all, Patrick had enough on his plate. "I hate hospitals too," she confessed, staring out of the window at the rows of cars parked below.

"Hey, I don't weigh that much!" Laura cried as Scott tried the lift, mistimed it and failed. His legs buckled and they both collapsed on the floor.

It was Saturday evening. They had met up in the gym down the road from Laura's house. Scott was dressed in trackie bottoms and his usual cool T-shirt, Laura wore a leotard under her sweatshirt.

"Show me again," Scott said. "Hang on. You take three steps towards me, I bend my knee, you step up and I use your forward motion to lift you onto my shoulder and you do your dying swan thing. Is that it?"

"Forget the dying swan. This has to be upbeat, loads of energy. Are you ready?"

Taking a deep breath, Scott nodded.

"Promise not to drop me?" she checked. "I don't want to go shooting straight over your shoulder and fall on my face!"

He nodded again, his face tense. He bent one knee in preparation. "Go ahead!"

Laura ran and stepped neatly onto Scott's knee. He put both hands on her waist and lifted her onto his shoulder, where she balanced, one leg bent, the other fully extended. She threw back her head and spread her arms like a bird in flight. "Okay, now put me down!"

Scott wobbled and almost overbalanced. Laura collapsed like a sack of potatoes over his shoulder. He staggered and let her slither to the floor. "You never told me how to put you down!" he gasped.

"Oops!" Laura rolled away then sprang to her feet, tugging at her ponytail and straightening her top. The session wasn't going too badly, considering. They were both working hard to get things right.

"Hey, how did your football match go?" she asked, waiting for him to recover his balance.

"We won, two-nil." Scott was in a good

mood, grinning at the fiasco of the failed lift.

"Cool," Laura smiled back. "Now maybe we could try this move one more time!"

CHAPTER 5

"How come you're so good at sports?" Laura asked Scott while they took a break from the ice during a practice session the following morning.

She wiped moisture off her skates as they sat in the café, overlooking the busy rink. Scott was due to leave at midday to get to afternoon football-coaching on time. "You've got to be good at something," he shrugged. "And I tell you for sure, I'm not winning any science or maths prizes, and according to my English teacher no way will I ever write a best seller!"

"You don't care, do you?" Laura had already picked up that he was totally laid back. Nothing seemed to bother him.

"Nope. It drives my dad crazy. He thinks I ought to work harder. On the whole, Dad's cool though. He comes to watch me play football every Saturday – he hasn't missed a match in two years!"

"And is he okay about you doing this training with me?" Laura wanted to know.

Scott nodded. "He says I'm living the life he always dreamed of for himself. His attitude is 'Go for it!'"

"That's brilliant. It's my mum more than my dad who's into the skating stuff." Laura took a sip of her drink, waggling her ankles and flexing her shoulders so she didn't stiffen up. "She's the one who drives me to competitions. But they're both pretty easy-going, actually." Not like Patrick's parents, who never stopped pushing him.

Scott nodded, biting into a chocolate bar and aiming the wrapper at the nearest bin. He scored a direct hit. "So what keeps you going? I mean, you're telling me we have to be up before dawn every single day if we want to get ready for this contest. That's a whole month of not enough sleep for me, but you must have been doing that forever!"

"Since I was eight," she admitted. She thought for a while. "I suppose I keep going because I just love it!"

"But *what* exactly?"

"I don't know. What do you love about football?"

"Hey, I just mess around. I can kick a ball better than the next kid, I guess."

Laura shook her head. "I don't believe that. I think that, deep down, you love the game. Like, I'm totally happy when I'm on the ice, like I'm flying or soaring. I love every second."

Scott grinned. "Maybe."

"Yes!" she insisted. "You're scared to say it, but you LOVE football! You work hard at it, you put in every bit of energy to play well – I could tell you do from the way you said you won two-nil."

He got up and made for the metal stairs.

"Maybe," he called over his shoulder. "But don't ever tell anyone I said that!"

"Wow, look at Scott!" The cry went up when he and Laura took to the ice to practise their paso doble. "Hey, that's not hip hop – what is it?"

"We've got to get our leg swings exactly together," Laura insisted, ignoring the remarks. "And when I turn away from you to go into my spin, you have to skate backwards and then curve round to meet me."

"Just watch, I'll crash into someone," Scott warned, glancing over his shoulder.

"Stay out of his way," a kid said, clearing the space for him and Laura.

"Ready?" Scott checked.

She nodded, counting out the beat of the music. One, two, three. Off they went, stepping across the ice, high-kicking then turning in opposite directions. Laura gathered her arms to spin. Scott sped backwards and then curved round to join her.

"Did you see that?" a mate of Scott's called out. "Their feet went up higher than their heads. Whoa, baby!"

"Good!" Laura nodded, catching Scott's hand and skating on. "Now let's try the lift."

He looked doubtfully at her. So far, though they'd worked it out in the gym, they hadn't tried it on ice. "Sure?"

Laura knew this was no time to stop, think and grow scared. "Yeah, let's try."

"Three steps, then you crook your right leg towards your chest. I catch you by the waist and raise you to my shoulder."

"You got it."

"Okay, let's do it."

Skating apart, knowing that all eyes were on them, Scott and Laura prepared for the lift. "One, two, three!" She tapped her hip to set up the tempo then set off across the ice. *Skate fast, hope that he gets hold of me, use the speed, soar through the air . . .*

There was a look of panic on Scott's face

as Laura sped towards him. Then he locked into her rhythm and timing, caught hold of her and hoisted her up onto his shoulder. "We did it!" he muttered, sailing on across the ice.

"Did you see it?" the watching kids gasped. "How cool was that?"

There was a wave of excitement; a couple of people clapped.

Scott skated on, lowering Laura to the ground, then heaved a sigh of relief. "Are you okay?" he asked.

She nodded, a grin splitting her face from ear to ear. "Cool!" she said. "It felt good. I knew you could do it."

"Yeah, go Scott!" other kids cheered.

There was only one person there who didn't look happy, and that was Will, sitting in the café with another football mate, looking down at Scott and Laura's antics on the ice. "What's he playing at?" he muttered. "Scott told me he wasn't going to do this. It's way out of order."

"How come?" Charlie Stone asked. "It looked okay to me."

Will shook his head. "It's not okay, dummy. It's scary stuff."

Charlie disagreed. "What's scary about dancing?"

"At fifty miles an hour, wearing a pair of knife-sharp blades on your feet?!" Will retorted. "If they had an accident, Scott could really hurt himself."

The two boys watched as Laura took their mate to one side and coached him, preparing for the next lift. Then Will got up. "I'm out of here," he told Charlie. "If Scott Yorke wants to wreck his chances of a career in premiership football, why should I care?"

CHAPTER 6

"Laura, I'm confused." Helen Lee came up to Laura's room later that night. "I just picked up a phone message from Vera, saying she can meet you at seven tomorrow morning."

"Good." Laura ducked her head half under the duvet and tried to sound sleepy.

"But why did you ask her to do that?" Laura's mum hadn't expected to be on taxi duty now that Patrick was injured. "What's the point of carrying on training without your partner?"

Laura disappeared further from sight. She didn't want to tell anyone about Scott until after Vera had seen him and confirmed that he was good enough to be Laura's partner.

It would be like jinxing their chances.
"Mum, I'm tired!"

"So you want me to drive you in?"

"Please, if you don't mind."

"And you don't think you should take it easy – do something else for a change, allow yourself to get over the disappointment of Montreal?"

Yawn, turn over, sound half-asleep. "No, I want to carry on training."

Helen nodded. "Okay," she agreed, closing the door softly behind her.

"I'm a bit worried about Laura," she confessed to her husband when she went downstairs. "She's all keyed up and on edge. I don't think she's taking Patrick's accident at all well."

Next day, Laura was the first to arrive at the rink.

"I'll stay and watch if you want," her mum offered, handing Laura her sports bag from the boot of the car.

"No thanks!" Laura hurried off towards the entrance with its unlit neon sign and scattering of loose tickets that littered the foyer. Her plan was to meet up with Vera and talk to her before Scott showed up.

He'll probably be late, she thought anxiously. *Scott's not the type to get here on time!*

So she hung about in the entrance, watching out for the coach's familiar fur hat and bright pink padded jacket, which she wore all year round.

Vera soon pulled up in her red car, stepping out and striding towards the entrance, surprised to see Laura lurking there. "Why aren't you changed, ready to warm up?" she asked.

"I wanted to explain something before we start." Walking through the foyer, Laura felt her pulse start to race. What she was about to say didn't sound convincing, even to her.

Vera shrugged. "Darling, it's okay if you want to carry on training without Patrick.

I admire your dedication — it's how champions are made."

"No, that's not what I meant . . ."

"There's plenty of work you can do on your own. We can improve your footwork without him."

"No, Vera — listen!" Laura jogged to keep up with her coach's long stride. She'd heard the door open behind them and guessed that Scott had just arrived. "I want to tell you something."

"Hey, Laura!" Scott called. "Sorry I'm late."

Vera turned with a puzzled expression. Then she faced Laura.

Laura grimaced. *This isn't how it was meant to happen. I was meant to set things up and convince her before Scott got here.* But here they were, Scott and Vera, face to face. "Vera, this is Scott Yorke. Scott, meet Vera Mozer!"

"Just run that by me again!" the coach said in disbelief.

Scott, Laura and Vera stood by the side of the rink, under the glaring lights.

Before Laura could answer, Vera held up a well-manicured hand. "No, forget that. Let me repeat what I think I just heard you say! Laura, you want Scott to be your new partner. Scott, you want me to work with you on our routines and get you ready in time for Montreal."

Laura nodded. She kept her fingers firmly crossed behind her back. "I know it's a bit unexpected," she murmured.

"Darling, do you want to give me a heart attack?" Vera looked Scott up and down then turned back to Laura. "It's impossible!"

"Okay, no worries, I'm out of here," Scott shrugged, readily doing an about-turn. No way did he like the look of Vera Mozer, who seemed to be even tougher than his football coach.

Laura panicked. "No, wait! Listen, Vera, you haven't seen Scott skate. He's really good!"

"He could be a genius for all I care." Vera shook her head and put up both hands in protest. "It's a crazy idea, Laura. We only have four weeks. No way is it going to work."

"Yeah, it's crazy," Scott agreed, taking the easy way out and setting off for the foyer.

Laura ran after him, then darted back to Vera. "You're not even giving me a chance!" she cried. "We've been working together all weekend. At least take a look at what we can do!"

Vera frowned, glancing towards Scott's rapidly disappearing figure. Then she looked hard at Laura, seeing the determination she knew so well. "You're serious, aren't you?"

"Totally. He's good, Vera. He's played ice-hockey. He learns fast."

"He has a good physique," the coach admitted. "Tall and strong for his age. A natural athlete."

Ignoring their discussion, Scott swung through the door and left the building.

"Please!" Laura begged. This meant more to her than anything in her entire life.

Vera tilted her head back and slowly brought it forward again. "Go bring him back," she agreed. "Let's see what he can do."

"Don't be nervous, okay!" Laura stood with Scott in the centre of the rink. She'd had to work hard to persuade him to come back and face Vera.

"What's to be nervous about?" he said with a self-mocking grin. "I'm only about to make an idiot of myself!"

"Paso doble — remember the rhythm, keep in time to the music, do all the arm stuff like I showed you." Laura waited for Vera to play the music, her heart in her mouth.

"Yeah," Scott muttered. He still wasn't keen on Scary Lady in her fur hat.

The notes started and they went smoothly into the routine, keeping perfect time and synchronising every step. Together they swung their legs and turned, together they spun, then Scott went down onto one knee to continue the spin, while Laura kicked her leg high over his head.

"Hm!" Vera said from the side of the ice.

Now they were up, hands linked and gliding on. It was time for the step sequence followed by the lift.

"Ready?" Laura said under her breath.

"Babe, this is fun!" Scott grinned back. The steps went perfectly then he split off from her in a wide curve.

Three steps and up, flying through the air, soaring along in a perfect lift!

Scott carried Laura close to where Vera stood then lowered her to the ice. They skated the final steps together.

"So?" Laura and Scott said together.

The coach couldn't disguise her amazement. Her eyes were wide and her mouth hung open as she stared from one to the other. Then she blinked and stared again.

"What do you think?" Laura prompted.

Vera cleared her throat, shaking her head as if trying to dismiss what she'd seen. "I don't believe it," she said.

"Well – do I stay or do I go?" Scott asked, seeing the funny side as always.

"Don't joke," Vera told him. "Ice dance is serious. Laura has pinned her hopes on you."

"Sorry." He lowered his head to hide his grin of triumph.

"Can we do it?" Laura asked. "Do you think we can get Scott ready for Montreal?"

The great coach spread her hands and raised her eyebrows before she gave her verdict. "We can try," she said at last.

CHAPTER 7

"No one said it would be easy," Laura reminded Scott.

They were four days into their official training with Vera, spending every minute they could on the ice. Their muscles ached, their bodies were bruised and battered. Now they sat together in the café, huddled over hot chocolate and cake.

"Yeah but no one said it would be this hard either." Two days earlier, Scott had brought his dad to meet Vera and they'd made the arrangements to get him measured and fitted out with his own top-class skates. Now he was wearing them and they were giving him blisters.

"Harder than football training?" she asked.

"Different. At footie training you're part of a gang, having a laugh. With Vera, every second is deadly serious."

Today, for instance, she had pulled Scott up a thousand times – "More lift and extension on the left leg . . . watch your posture . . . control your feet!"

"Don't let Vera get to you," Laura said, picking up what he was thinking. "I know she seems really strict, but she's a cool teacher."

"She's a slave driver," he complained. "I reckon she never says anything nice, even if you're dying out there."

Taking a big bite of cake, unable to deny what he'd just said, Laura sat and thought for a while about how she could help Scott through this first week. They were starting by learning the compulsory paso doble before they moved on to the original programme of salsa and rumba. "Look at it this way," she told him, "if you can survive four weeks of Vera, you get to go to Canada."

"Hey, maybe I'll get to see some ice hockey!" Scott's eyes lit up. "Cool!"

"Plus, we're there with a chance of a medal, remember!" Okay, so there was still a mountain of work to get through that was as steep as a ski-slope, but Laura hadn't given up hope of the bronze at least.

Unluckily for her, their conversation was interrupted by the arrival of Will, Charlie and a bunch of Scott's other mates. They crowded round, demanding to know how the routines were going.

"Hey, Scott, how are the pirouettes coming?" Will asked, enjoying putting his friend under pressure. He hadn't forgiven him for lying to him about not doing the wussy ice-dance stuff. "Did you get your ballet costume sorted out yet?"

Scott sniffed and sat with a blank expression.

"Come on, what colour are your tights?" Will joked. He was a tough-looking kid with scruffy, mouse-brown hair and a top lip that lifted readily into a scoffing grin.

"We don't do pirouettes and boys don't wear tights for ice dance!" Laura said, putting Will right. "Listen, give us a break, will you?"

"Tip-tip-tip, tippety-toe!" Will jeered, mimicking a ballet dancer and making everyone laugh.

On top of the bruises and recent falls, this was more than Scott could take. "Jeez!" he said, scraping back his chair and walking away. He disappeared into the toilets, to the sound of his mates' laughter.

Laura frowned and glared at Will, who sat down opposite her. "Thanks!"

Will pushed out his bottom lip and shrugged. "Don't mention it."

"I keep telling you, this isn't funny. Anyway, what's wrong with Scott coming to Canada? Why are you trying to spoil it for him?"

At first Will denied it, but as Scott

reappeared and toughed it out with his other mates, Will suddenly got serious with Laura. "Think about it," he said, leaning across the table towards her. "Tell me what happened with your first partner – Patrick what's-his-name. He had an accident, didn't he?"

Laura narrowed her eyes and nodded. She could already see where this was leading.

"I hear he broke his kneecap." Will leaned back in his chair, slowly shaking his head. "What if that happens to Scott? Where does that leave him?"

"I don't know, you tell me."

"It leaves him with no contract for United Juniors, which is what he's aiming for at the start of next season. If he breaks a leg, he's finished!"

Laura took a deep breath then sighed. She stood up and walked away. "He won't break his leg!" she muttered to herself. "He'll win a medal, you'll see!"

★ ★ ★

"Keep a clean line, Scott. No, that's not good enough. Try again!" Vera kept picking on him over and over again, through the weekend and into the early part of the following week.

Laura demonstrated the moves, aware that her mum was standing beside Vera, keeping a close eye on what was going on.

"Show me that again?" Scott asked Laura.

She went into a combination spin, stopped and got Scott to copy her.

"I don't get it," he muttered, coming out of it and shaking his head.

"Watch, it's easy." Again she did the move, then watched him copy her. Scott wobbled and looked dizzy as he came to a halt.

"We haven't got all day!" Vera shouted across the ice. Impatient though she was at the best of times, working with Scott seemed to be making her temper even worse.

Laura noticed her mum lean over and speak to the coach. "Yeah, tell her to give us a break!" she muttered under her breath. She nodded as Scott rehearsed the spin again and finally got it. "The salsa has to have lots of fast spins," she explained. "But once you've got used to the speed, it all comes pretty smoothly."

"Says you!" Today there was no joking, no fun in it as far as he was concerned. "Doesn't Scary Woman ever let up?"

Laura shook her head. "But underneath, she's cool. She cares."

"Yeah, about reliving her glory days by getting us to win another gold medal for her," Scott grumbled, deep in the doldrums. "I reckon it's not actually us she cares about."

Laura skated backwards, circling around while Vera decided what they should do next. She frowned as she thought about what Scott had just said, then she came back to join him. "That's not true," she decided. "I know Vera seems strict, but . . ."

"Heart of ice. Ice Queen!" Scott insisted,

glancing at the two women by the barrier.

". . . But no, underneath she's kind. I've seen it. I know she is!"

Laura's serious expression brought the old smile to Scott's face. "I believe you!" he grinned. "Like, yeah, I really do!"

The second week of training did not get easier as it went on. For a start, Scott and Laura had taken more falls than usual. Their skates had clicked together during a step sequence and brought them down, sending them skidding over the ice on their backs. Then Scott had lost control of the combination spin in the salsa and ended up pulling Laura down. And so it went on.

Besides, Vera's mood had worsened. By the end of the week she was so gloomy that even Laura was beginning to think her idea of finding a new partner had been a mistake.

And now, at ten-thirty on Friday evening,

as Scott and Laura collapsed, exhausted, on the bench at the side of the rink, Laura's mobile went off and she saw Patrick's name come up on the tiny screen.

"Hi, Patrick!" she said, trying to sound more cheerful than she felt. "How are you?"

Scott leaned back against the row of chairs behind him, legs stretched out, arms hanging by his sides.

". . . Yeah, I'm fine, thanks." Quickly Laura picked up a note of worry in Patrick's voice. ". . . I'm at the ice rink. Why do you ask?"

"Okay, Scott, that's enough for today," Vera was telling him. "Go home to bed."

Laura listened to the voice on the phone for a while then spoke again. ". . . Yeah, actually, that's true. How did you find out? . . . No, of course I wasn't trying to hide it from you . . . No, don't worry. Yeah, I would have told you soon . . ."

"What's up?" Scott asked, glad to be left alone by Vera, who had walked off to speak to Laura's mum.

". . . Honestly, Patrick, I'm not going behind your back. And whatever your dad's told you, this really isn't a permanent thing. No . . . yes. I'm sorry. Bye." She sighed and sagged forward as she ended the call.

"So, that was Patrick!" Scott groaned. Every time he moved, a new muscle ached. "Sounds to me like you're in trouble."

"I should have been upfront before now and told him I was working with a new partner," Laura sighed again. "Only I was waiting for the right moment, and now his dad has somehow found out and broken the news to him out of the blue."

"Yeah, I guessed." By now Scott was sitting up and paying attention. "So Patrick's not happy?"

Laura shook her head. She felt terrible about the phone conversation she'd just had.

There was a long silence, with them both staring out across the empty rink, before Scott spoke again. "You know what?" he said. "I'm thinking this might not be such a great idea, after all."

Laura's heart jumped but she tried to hold her voice steady. "Hey, come on," she coaxed. "I'll visit Patrick and put him in the picture. He won't mind in the end."

"It's not just that. There's all this work, and I haven't finished learning the original section yet. We haven't even started on the free dance."

"We have over two weeks left. You can do it!" Laura felt her stomach churn. She was afraid that Scott was on the point of walking away.

"Then there's Scary Woman," he muttered. "It's no fun when you've got her on your back, day in, day out!"

"I don't think it's Patrick, or the work, or Vera," Laura challenged. "I think what's really bugging you is Will!"

"That's stupid!" Scott stood up and collected his skates. He was in a big sulk with Laura because she'd seen through his excuses and hit the nail on the head. No way did he want his mates laughing at him and making fun of him. "Anyway, whatever. I'm out of here!"

Laura joined her mum, feeling as though her world had ended. Scott had walked out on her. She had no partner for Montreal.

Helen Lee took one look at her daughter and marched her straight to the car. "No need to talk," she said. "Let me guess – Scott has changed his mind?"

Miserably Laura nodded. "In a way, I don't blame him."

"Shh." Her mum steered the car out of the car park. "I knew Vera was putting too much pressure on him. I had a word with her about it a few days ago."

"I know, Mum. Thanks. But it wasn't just that. I mean, Scott's laidback really – he just wants to have fun. But he can work hard as well, and he was getting really good."

"So what made him change his mind?"

Sitting in the traffic, Helen glanced at Laura and saw the weary tears trickling down her cheeks.

"Stupid stuff!" Laura sniffed. "Partly 'cos Patrick found out what was happening and threw a hissyfit."

"Which can be fixed," Helen pointed out. "We just have to explain that Scott is only your partner while Patrick is out of action. Then it'll be back to the old partnership of you and Patrick – won't it?"

Laura nodded. "Scott wants to play football for United. That's really his thing. I'll want to skate with Patrick again, once he's fit."

"So, no problem." Helen always found a positive way of seeing things. "What else?"

Laura got to the nitty-gritty. "Scott's footie mates are making fun of him. He can't take it."

"Now that really is daft!" Laura's mum eased through the lights and made a quick turn to the left. She pulled into a supermarket car park. "Ice dance is a tough discipline. It's not for wimps!"

"I know that, but stupid Will doesn't!"

Helen thought for a while. "It seems to me there's nothing here that can't be fixed, Laura. Listen to me – this is what we're going to do!"

CHAPTER 8

While Laura's mum went to see Mr and Mrs Cole to explain the real situation, Laura sat at home and texted Scott: *Need 2 c u now.*

She waited five minutes for a reply, then sent a second message: *Ansa me!!!*

One more minute and then a reply arrived. *Nothing 2 say. Bye!*

Still need 2 c u!

Go away – end of story.

"Says who?" Laura muttered, switching to direct action. She punched in Scott's number and waited for him to answer.

"Don't you get it, Laura? Leave me alone!" He came straight at her as soon as he answered the phone. "I'm up to here with double twists and triple throw loops. I never want to hear another salsa as long as I live!"

"Tell me where you live. I need to talk to you, face to face."

Scott couldn't believe what he was hearing. "Are you deaf? Or just crazy?"

Laura laughed. "Crazy, I guess! You have to be, to do what I do!"

"I knew it!" Scott laughed back. "I'm dealing with Crazy Girl."

"And Scary Woman," she reminded him. "Listen, I've had an idea. No one knows about it yet − not even Vera. But I need to see you to talk it over. Come on, tell me − where do you live?"

There was a long pause. "If I see you now, do you promise not to stalk me for the rest of my life?"

"Yeah, promise!"

"And just for five minutes, okay?"

"Five minutes." She grinned as Scott gave her the address. "Cool. That's only ten minutes from here on foot. Wait there. Bye!"

"Five minutes, then *adios*." Scott opened the door warily to let Laura in. He was still in his tracksuit bottoms but had thrown on an old United shirt which he wore around the house. "So what's new?"

Laura breezed into the hallway. "Mum's gone round to the Coles' place to calm them down. I've come here to talk about our free dance section."

"*Our* free dance section?" he echoed. "There is no "our", remember?"

"But there will be, after you've listened to this," she said briskly. "Okay, so it's risky and no one's ever done anything like this before, but once the judges get their heads around it, they'll see it's really cool, and if we get it right, they'll give it top marks – you've got to believe me!"

"Whoa, whoa, whoa!" Scott backed off against the telephone table. "What are you talking about, Crazy Girl?"

"*Our* free dance," she insisted. "The third component – it's the part where we get to do our own thing to one long piece of music – you know, the Torvill and Dean dying-swan bit."

Scott shook his head wearily. "I don't know where this is going," he groaned, "but just spit it out, will you?"

"Okay." Laura's eyes sparkled. She'd got back all her energy and enthusiasm. "The couples who will be skating in Montreal – they'll all be dancing to waltz music, or sambas or cha-cha-chas – stuff that everybody expects. But it came to me in a flash – why don't we do something completely different? Something modern and funky that nobody ever did before?"

"Like what?" Scott frowned, still trying to guess what was coming.

"You'll like it!" she promised. "At first I thought jive, or rock and roll – you know, real 1950s stuff. But other ice-dance couples already do that. Then I thought, why not get even more modern – why not street music, why not hip hop?"

"Now you're seriously crazy," Scott muttered, turning to show her to the door.

"Wait! Hip hop, with really cool, loud music which you can choose. And you'll have to teach me the moves over the next couple of days, and next week Vera will make it fit the Grand Prix requirements, with all the lifts and spins and stuff thrown in . . ."

"Hmm!" Scott started to give Laura's idea some serious thought. "Would it be allowed?" he double-checked.

She nodded eagerly. "Think about it – if we dance hip hop, none of your mates will be able to make fun of us. In fact, even Will has to think it's cool."

"I'm already cool," Scott reminded her. "Or I was – until you came along!"

"Okay, I'll be cool too. C'mon, Scott, hip hop, street rhythms, funky music – how can you say no?"

"Huh!" he said, looking at Laura as if she was a little less crazy than he'd thought. He pictured them on the ice, mirroring moves, getting into the spirit of hip hop and breakdancing. "You know, that might just work!"

Laura felt relief spread over her like a warm shower. Her face relaxed into a bright smile. "So will you?" she asked.

Scott nodded. "I guess Crazy Girl has talked me into it," he said.

Next morning at the ice rink, during the public session, Laura explained to Scott that they didn't want to hit their coach full in the face with their hip-hop idea. "Music-wise, Vera's stuck in the seventies and eighties," she told him. "If we said we were doing Abba, she'd be fine."

They both broke into a version of 'Knowing Me, Knowing You!', sang a few bars, then burst out laughing.

Other kids around the rink took up the

song and began to do eighties dance moves on the ice.

"We have to go behind her back and work on some moves today," Laura went on. "But I'm relying on you. I don't have a clue how to begin."

Scott grinned and told her to switch on the track. He had brought in an iPod loaded with the track he'd chosen, and speakers.

"For a start, we've got to get the rhythm." He started moving to the fast, strong beat with broken rhythms and scratch sounds, attracting a small crowd, including Laura's friend, Abi, and Scott's mate, Laura's major enemy, Will.

Laura copied Scott and soon some of the others joined in, but when Scott dropped low and went into a spin on one leg, only Laura followed. Abi tried it but quickly overbalanced and fell. "The beat is too fast!" she cried, picking herself up.

Coming out of the spin, Scott sprang forward into a handstand.

"Uh-oh, no!" Laura ground to a halt, hands on her hips. "Ice-dance rules won't let us put our hands on the ice."

Scott stopped and thought again. "What about a step sequence like this?"

Once more he demonstrated and Laura copied. "Cool!" she said, a big smile spreading over her face. They strung together the opening arm movements, the spin and the steps.

"Hip hop!" Abi grinned and clapped. "Is this for your programme in Montreal?"

Laura nodded. "Top secret. Don't tell anyone!"

"Fat chance," Will muttered. "There's only twenty people standing here watching!"

She ignored him. "We can spin on our knees, do high kicks, I can slide between your legs, you can swing your leg over my head, anything except touch the ice with our hands."

"And we need a few lifts?" Scott checked.

She nodded. "Some straight, some

rotational. The harder the better, 'cos we score higher for degree of difficulty. But for now, I think we have to get the opening sequence right, so we can show Vera what we've been working on."

For a few minutes they rehearsed the moves, getting them smoother and more synchronised. Laura loved the fast, funky rhythm and threw herself into the flowing hip-hop style, following Scott's every move.

"That looks great!" Abi encouraged, and even Will stopped scowling and added a suggestion or two of his own.

"Hey, throw in a dance-off. Scott, you do your thing then challenge Laura to go one better. Y'know, breakdance stuff!"

"Cool!" Gradually Scott and Laura were clearing a bigger space on the ice and attracting more kids. Everyone was clapping as the pair took up Will's idea and tried to out-dance each other.

Laura watched Scott do a diagonal step

sequence with a couple of turns and a low, crouching spin. She took him on with a slow, funky series of turning steps, ending in a double twist.

"Go, Laura!" the girls cried.

"Go, Scott!" the boys replied.

Grinning and laughing, they danced themselves to a standstill, while the little kids took over the ice and tried to copy the simpler moves.

"What do you think?" Scott asked Will as they headed for the barrier to take a rest. He badly wanted to bring his mate on side.

There was a long pause. Will went through his own struggle with pride and resentment, and his serious worries that Scott could get injured. "I think bling," he said in the end.

"Meaning?"

"Meaning, forget the sequins, go for bling."

"Are you talking costumes?" Laura checked.

The tough soccer star of tomorrow nodded. "Big gold chains, bro. Plenty of chest on show."

"Does that mean you think it's cool now?" Scott asked, grinning at Laura behind his mate's back.

Will grunted then nodded. "Go for it, dude. Go to Montreal. This stuff will knock 'em senseless!"

Laura felt that she'd climbed a high mountain in the past two and half weeks and was nearing the top. The summit was in sight.

Okay, she'd hit a few obstacles – the odd sheer rock face that looked unclimbable, the unsuspected crevasse and occasional avalanche that had sent her sliding into the depths. But now, with Scott back on board and everyone at the rink telling them that the hip-hop programme was a brilliant idea, her hopes were high.

"Well done, Laura, I'm pleased for you,"

her mum told her that night, coming into her room to tell her it was time for lights out. "You've shown real guts to get this far after Patrick had his accident."

"The main thing was persuading Scott to stick with it," Laura explained. For once she was ready to go to sleep, her body exhausted after her day at the rink. "But now we've got this really cool programme for the free dance which we're going to show Vera tomorrow."

Helen nodded. "Like I said, you've given it everything you've got. So what's the new programme? Is it going to be waltz, or something a bit more up-tempo?"

"Up-tempo," Laura smiled, deliberately keeping the secret until after she and Scott had showed Vera their ideas.

"Laura, what aren't you telling me?"

"Surprise!" Laura laughed and snuggled under her duvet. "Wait until tomorrow morning, then you'll see!"

CHAPTER 9

"I've altered the details on the plane tickets for Montreal," Vera told Scott first thing the following morning. "I've given the airline your name instead of Patrick's. Everything's fine."

They'd met early, as usual, at a time when the rink was opened specially for them. Vera was dressed as always in her fur hat and pink padded jacket, Scott and Laura in their practice gear. Scott had brought in his hip-hop CD, which he had tucked away under the player on Vera's folding rink-side table.

"Anyway, no time to stand and chat," Vera said briskly. "Scott, did you get your blades sharpened like I told you?"

He nodded, feeling more nervous than usual.

"Did you warm up, both of you?" the coach asked.

"Before you got here," Laura said.

"So, we begin to think today about our free programme," Vera went on. "Scott, I want to teach you the same programme we had for Patrick. Laura knows it already, which means she can help you to learn."

Laura wrinkled her nose and twitched her mouth to one side. "Erm . . ."

"It's a very classical piece," Vera went on. "Everything must flow to a waltz time. It requires grace and control."

"Actually . . ." Laura interrupted. She was trying to figure out how to explain. *Don't hit her in the face with it,* she reminded herself. *Break it to her gently.*

But Scott charged in like a bull in a china shop. "Watch this!" he told Vera, sliding the CD into the player before grabbing Laura by the hand and skating into the centre of the ice.

Vera stood by the side of the ice, her mouth wrinkled like a prune, wondering what was going on.

The breakdance music shattered the silence of the vast space with an explosion of drumbeats and scratchy keyboard sounds. Scott and Laura took up the broken rhythms and went into their opening sequence.

"Forget classical!" Scott muttered. "Try hip hop instead!"

"My God!" Vera cried, putting her hands to her ears. "What is this?"

Rushed into their dance without preparation, Laura had to throw caution to the winds. *Okay, this is it!* she told herself. *Vera is either gonna hate it or love it!*

She and Scott snaked their hips and strutted, spun and stepped until their coach suddenly stopped the music.

"What is this dreadful noise?" Vera demanded, turning to Helen Lee who had just come in. "What is Laura thinking of?"

Laura's mum shook her head. "It's news to me."

Laura took a deep breath and gritted her teeth. "I knew it. We should've broken it to her more gently!"

But Scott skated across to where the two women stood. "It's street music – breakdance, hip hop – all the kids are playing it!"

"I don't care. It's disgusting!" Vera insisted, pulling a face as if she'd just swallowed live maggots. "What is wrong with a classical waltz or quickstep?"

"That's for old people," Scott told her, while Laura winced. "And we're not old, we're young. This is a *junior* championship, remember."

"Laura, what are you thinking?" Vera cried. "Have you forgotten everything I've taught you?"

At last, Laura found her voice. "You have to give us a chance," she insisted. "At least watch us again. Let us get through to the end of the sequence."

"That's fair enough," Helen agreed. "Let's not write it off without thinking about it properly."

Vera tutted and frowned. "I never heard anything like this music. It sounds like mice scratching around inside a tin drum!"

"But just watch this!" Eagerly Laura skated ahead of Scott onto the ice and took up her starting position. This time she was ready to throw herself into the routine.

It was her mum who re-started the track.

Once more the hip-hop rhythms broke the silence. Scott went into the dance-off section with a stunning spin then down into the splits. Laura came back with a double lutz then joined hands with Scott and they set off at high speed on a diagonal sequence ending in a combination spin.

"Wow!" Helen Lee was taken aback. "That is actually pretty spectacular," she murmured.

The two women watched keenly, taking in every step and turn. When the music ended, Vera sighed and beckoned the skaters to her.

"So?" Laura gasped. She knew they'd danced well, but had they convinced their coach?

"Very original," Vera said, a deep frown-line forming between her eyebrows. "But ugly."

"No!" Laura protested. "This is what kids like to dance to."

"We do," Scott agreed, looking from Vera to Helen and then back again.

"Ugly . . . but clever," Vera added, obviously thinking deeply. "And very, very risky."

"That's what we want to do – we want to take a risk!" Laura pleaded. "I've got a new partner. I'd like to do something no one ever did before!"

"Hmm." Still the coach turned it over in her mind. "What about the judges? Are they ready? You know it could be a disaster in their eyes."

Slowly Laura breathed out then in again.

"It's athletic. It looks fantastic − doesn't it, Mum?"

Helen backed off from the group. "Not my decision," she said quietly.

"Athletic − yes," Vera agreed. "It's a style that's suited to show off what the boy in the partnership can do as well as the girl. And we could work in some sensational lifts . . ."

"Say yes," Laura begged. This was the last big obstacle. If Vera refused, she didn't know what she would do.

Vera closed her eyes, opened them again and nodded. "We will set the world of ice dance on fire!" she agreed. "We will do something brand new."

"Oh fantastic!" Laura clasped her hands tightly together. Her eyes sparkled. "Oh Vera, thank you!"

"But!" Their coach held up a warning finger. "Laura and Scott, if we are to win, you must work harder than you have ever worked before!"

★ ★ ★

Work, work, work – every waking minute of the week and a half before the Montreal championships, Laura lived and dreamed ice-dance.

She and Scott learned lifts from Vera that they had never even thought of – one especially, where they skated back to back, elbows linked. Then Scott leant forward and Laura rolled onto his back. She had to swing both legs to her right and roll underneath him while he stood up straight and went into a spin. She then hooked her hands behind his neck and used their speed to fling her legs out behind her. All this was at high speed, so that Laura was aware at times of her face dipping so close to the ice that her cheeks were sprinkled with the white powder rising from Scott's sharp blades.

"Ooh!" Onlookers gasped and breathed a sigh of relief when Laura landed safely.

Meanwhile, Helen talked to Scott and

Laura about costumes for the free dance.

"Will said bling," Laura reminded him. "But we can't wear chunky gold chains – they'd swing all over the place and be dangerous."

"We can have gold fabric medallion shapes sewn into the tops," Helen suggested. "Laura, do you want to wear a skirt or trousers?"

"Trousers!" Her answer was instant. "Black. And a black crop-top with a logo. We need our costumes to look like a version of what hip-hop kids wear, not all floaty chiffon and frills."

"How about baseball caps?" Scott asked.

Vera groaned and walked away. "What was I thinking of, saying yes to this?" she muttered.

"Maybe not the caps?" Helen suggested tactfully.

"No caps," Laura agreed. Better not to push it too hard. After all, dear old Vera had already come a long way.

★ ★ ★

Work and sleep. Work and sleep. They were one day from taking the plane to Montreal. And that was when Patrick arrived at the rink to watch Scott and Laura work.

They were rehearsing the free dance in their new costumes – mostly black with shiny gold trimming around the neck and wrists, cut to look like funky street clothes, complete with hoods. Laura's hair was tied back in a high, spiky ponytail.

Quietly Patrick limped up and stood next to Vera. Helen Lee joined them.

"Hi, Patrick. Fasten your seatbelt and watch this!" Laura's mum warned.

From the ice, Laura spotted Patrick's arrival. She felt sad for him on his crutches, still looking pale and a bit thinner than before. She waved and gave him a thumbs-up sign.

Then, of course, the moment the first beat of the music played, she forgot everything except the dance. She counted the beat, snaked her hips and started.

The step sequences went perfectly in this, their last practice before they flew to Canada. They'd speeded everything up to keep perfect time. Vera had added a last-minute degree of difficulty here, and put in an extra spin there. *Yes!* Laura said to herself during the dance-off section. *This is beginning to feel like fun!* Even the big, difficult lift went perfectly.

Exhilarated, she and Scott struck their final pose, down on both knees, arms folded, out-staring their audience.

Then Laura sprang up and skated quickly towards Patrick. *Please say you liked it!* she thought.

Patrick gave a small shake of his head.

"What's wrong, are you in shock?" Laura tried to make a joke. *Oh God, he doesn't like it. He thinks we're mad!*

Her old partner stared at her new partner who had just skated alongside her, still out of breath, but with a grin all over his face. "Hey, Patrick!" he said brightly, but was met by a stunned silence.

It was Vera who stepped in and broke it. "Free dance!" she explained. "Something a little different."

"A *little* different!" Laura grinned awkwardly, desperate for Patrick to approve, yet knowing how hard this must be for him. "Scott looks so cool, doesn't he? He's worked so hard and done so well!"

The small frown that was creasing Patrick's brow slowly faded. "Not exactly what I expected," he muttered, shaking his head again. "I've only ever seen stuff like that on pop videos."

"But?" Laura prompted. If Patrick approved, she could step onto that plane with a spring in her step. She could dance in Montreal with a clear conscience.

"But amazing!" Patrick told her. He shook his head over and over, lost for words. "I don't believe it, it's so . . ."

". . . Cool?" Laura suggested.

Patrick nodded, starting to smile. "Cool!

New . . . exciting . . . stunning . . . it's unbelievable!"

"Thanks for saying that, Patrick — I'm so happy!" Laura exclaimed, giving him a first-time-ever hug.

"Yeah well, just win that medal," he told her, squirming with embarrassment. "Don't come back with bronze or silver. Remember, only the gold will do!"

CHAPTER 10

Abi and Georgina and the kids at school would never believe it, Laura thought, looking back on the day of the flight to Canada.

Here she was in her hotel bed, trying to get some sleep.

They'd never believe I've flown across the Atlantic without even looking out of the window or watching a movie on the personal screen. They'd say I'm seriously dumb not to have noticed the mountains, or to have got the autographs of a couple of famous ice-dancers we met on the bus from the airport to the hotel!

It had all happened in such a whirl — saying goodbye to Immy, Jimmy, Jack and her mum and dad at the airport, boarding the plane, even the flying, with Vera on one side and Scott in the window seat, going on about the mountains and rivers he could see way below.

And then they had landed and come through immigration clutching their hand luggage that contained their skating costumes. Then there was baggage reclaim, crowded with other skaters from their competition, arriving from eastern Europe and the United States. Vera had run into old friends and colleagues and talked non-stop on the bus, while both Scott and Laura were in a daze.

"Sleep!" Vera had instructed them both as soon as they'd had a meal in the hotel. "You must be ready mentally and physically for the compulsory dance tomorrow morning."

No time to think, no time to get nervous. Just sleep.

"Please let it go well tomorrow!" Laura murmured into the darkness. Bedtime felt like early the following day. Her body clock was all wrong. "Please let us not make any stupid mistakes. Let everything be as good as it can possibly be!"

"Is it always as bad as this?" Scott asked Laura as they watched the American junior champions come off the ice after their compulsory programme.

Laura nodded. "The waiting's the worst part." She and Scott had to skate second-to-last, hanging around until almost all the other couples had performed.

"I don't know how you stand it," he muttered. "My nerves are shot!"

"Shh!" Laura wanted to concentrate on the American score. They got 18.25 for technical merit, 18.63 for programme components. That put them in second place, behind the Italians. The American couple hugged their coach, then sat down to watch the next pair.

"Really, I mean it – this is killing me!" Scott whispered. His throat felt dry, his palms were sweating. "It's worse than any cup final!"

Laura managed a grin. "Remember to tell Will that!" she said. Now it was the turn of the Russians, dressed in scarlet from head to toe. They danced confidently, with perfectly matched leg lines and a seriously good curve lift.

"Too close to the boards on the serpentine steps," Vera muttered, ever critical.

There was a long wait for the scores. At last the announcement came: 18.49 and 19.07 – a total of 37.56, pushing them ahead of the Americans but still behind the Italians, who had achieved 38.20.

"How long now?" Scott groaned. The idea of being out on the ice in front of the huge crowd, with judges watching every move, scared the life out of him. "I want to get this over with, then curl up and die!"

"Tutt!" Vera clicked her tongue, telling Scott to lift up his skates so she could check his blades. "You can do this. Keep your focus. Don't let the nerves get to you."

I hope he can do it! Laura thought to herself. *Don't let us down, Scott!*

They watched two more couples dance before their own names were announced.

"Laura Lee and Scott Yorke for the United Kingdom!"

Laura felt the sudden thrill of her name being called. She took a deep breath, glanced at her partner, then skated smoothly out onto the ice.

This is it – paso doble! Think proud, think Latin – arch your back, lift your head, look like a Spanish princess!

Scott took up his position and the music began. He let it guide his movements, transforming his laidback posture into a fiery Latin, foot-stamping character.

Okay, good! Laura knew that she and Scott were exactly on the beat. She felt the strong overhead lights beat down on them, highlighting every step.

Halfway through and it was going well.

Her silver chiffon skirt fluttered around her legs as Scott made the first lift and she soared through the air like a shiny bird.

Cool! Now, keep away from the boards, pick up more speed, watch the right foot on the twizzle – not quite perfect – get back together for the three inside turns – better! Okay, now spin and strike a pose!

Before they knew it, the programme was over. The audience clapped. Someone in the crowd waved a giant British flag.

"Pretty good," Vera told them as they rejoined her and sat down for the anxious wait for their score.

The announcer spoke: 18.36 and 18.92!

"Third place!" Vera said.

Scott clenched his fists. Laura held her breath. Third after the compulsory section, behind Italy and Russia! As the final couple skated and failed to challenge the leaders, Laura bit her lip and shook her head in amazement. "Cool!" she whispered. "We're in with a real chance of a medal!"

★ ★ ★

It was weird what happened when you were on an adrenalin high. First, you could feel your heart racing. Second, you talked too fast and couldn't stop.

"Slow down!" Vera ordered Laura, dragging her away from the rink where the big Zamboni machine was sweeping about, resurfacing the ice. The coach took Laura and Scott for lunch. "You need to keep calm and save your strength for the original dance this afternoon."

The restaurant was crowded with competitors from around the world, many of whom had met before. They spoke English to one another, discussing the morning's performance, and all were eager to meet Laura's new partner.

"Where did you find him?" Nina Simakova asked Laura enviously. "He's too good!"

Scott blushed and carried on eating.

"I know." Laura smiled back. "I found

him at our local rink, actually!"

And the Russian girl grinned and went away, thinking that Laura had been kidding.

"Hey, I heard about Patrick's accident." Michelle Lamoureux came up next to give Scott the third degree. "Where did you learn to skate? How come the Brits have been hiding you away until now?"

"I learned at my local rink," he insisted. "Laura kind of forced me into this."

The Canadian girl laughed. "No way!"

"I'm serious."

"Wow!" Realizing that he really was serious, Michelle went off to tell some of the others.

Scott frowned and looked at Laura. "What am I – some kind of freak?"

It was her turn to laugh. She thought of how far he'd come, and how fast. "Nope, you're a skating superstar!" she told him. "But don't let it go to your head!"

"Okay, now, not too much drama, like with

the Italians," Vera warned them before they went out to skate the salsa routine.

We have to hold on to third place! Laura told herself. *I know we can do it — and maybe even go one better!*

The Italian pair had slipped to second place behind the Russians. America was pushing the UK hard from fourth place.

"Next to skate, Laura Lee and Scott Yorke, lying in third place for the United Kingdom!"

"Enjoy!" Vera whispered, launching them into their original programme.

Yeah, enjoy! Laura smiled at Scott. *How cool is this! Pinch me and tell me I'm not dreaming.*

The bright lights shone down. They were ready to begin.

Keep to the beat, keep a clean line, kick, turn, kick! Think about your balance, stay in time, go into the splits, come up and spin. Laura and Scott attacked their serpentine steps with loads of energy and fun.

Then they slowed for the rumba section,

leaning in, winding around each other, going into a smooth, silky lift as the trumpet sounded.

Shaky landing! Laura told herself. She felt her right skate wobble before she righted herself. But would the judges have noticed?

They sprang back into salsa rhythm, matching their steps and leg lines, covering the ice faster than they ever had before, ending with a low spin for Laura while Scott turned and swung his leg over her head.

They finished and skated towards Vera, whose blank expression gave nothing away.

"Did you see my bad landing?" Laura whispered, hardly daring to look up at the scoreboard.

The coach nodded.

"Hey, chill out," Scott said. "It was one tiny mistake!"

But it was enough to push them into fourth place and out of the medals for now. As the scores appeared, Laura's heart sank. "It was that stupid landing!" she muttered bitterly.

"Look what I did – I went and knocked us out of the bronze-medal position!"

CHAPTER 11

There was nothing for it that night but to go to bed and sleep on it.

Vera had done her best to talk Laura out of her bad mood, promising that everything would look different the following day. "Fourth place is good," she'd urged. "It means you still have everything to skate for."

"Yeah, look at us." Scott was still amazed by the whole scene. "We're dancing with the best in the world here. I mean, these kids have skill!"

But Laura still went to her room in a bad mood. She couldn't help blaming herself for her mistake, and when she spoke to her mum on the phone, she had to let her disappointment show.

"It wasn't Scott letting me down," she told her. "It was the other way around."

"Listen, I'm sure you're exaggerating," Helen replied. "You're not going to be 100 percent perfect through all three programmes – that's impossible."

"Yeah, but I was careless – it shouldn't have happened." Laura knew she shouldn't beat herself up and decided to try to sound more positive. "Anyway, maybe tomorrow we'll get through the whole thing without a mistake."

"That's better!" her mum said. "You know we'll all be thinking about you. Immy says to tell you good luck."

"Sweet!" Laura smiled then sighed. "Wish you were here, Mum."

"Me too, honey."

"Okay, then. I'll skate for you and Dad tomorrow. I'll make you proud."

"Laura, we are already as proud as could be! Now go to sleep. Oh, and tell

Scott good luck from us. Tell him we think he's amazing!"

"If you two pull this off, it will be the biggest surprise in ice-dance history!" Vera gave Scott and Laura their final pep talk. She had taken them to one side just seconds before they were due on the ice. "But remember, we are taking a big risk, and it might not pay off!"

"It will!" Laura gathered her courage by clenching her fists. The scores had just come up for Nina Simakova and her partner, Anton Kuznetsov. The Russians had pushed themselves into the lead. Now it was all down to Laura and Scott.

"It will be a big shock for the judges, remember." Wanting to prepare Laura, Vera laid it on the line. "We have made sure that all the components are within the rules, but the style is not what they expect."

Laura nodded. "I hear you." For a split second she felt doubt. Then she shut it out.

"Y'know what, Scott?"

"What?" he asked, hearing their names called and turning towards the bright rink.

Laura stepped onto the ice beside him, dressed in her blingy black crop-top and trousers. "We're definitely, 100 percent for sure going to make ice-dance history here today!"

The music began. A gasp went up in the audience.

"Come to the hip-hop jam, come to the jitterbug jam . . . at the hip-hop shop you don't stop . . ." Drums sounded the rhythm, one track cutting into another, the DJ dragging a record back and forth to cut and scratch and break and chop the rhythm.

Scott and Laura leaped into action, jerking their bodies to the broken beat, racing across the ice with a string of funky steps and jumps.

The audience fell silent. Was this serious? What were the UK dancers up to?

Laura sensed the confusion. *Hey!* she said to herself, *If we go down, at least we go down big time!*

Scott reached out for her hand and together they went into a series of twizzles before they went back to back and linked elbows to go into the level-four lift. Laura rolled off Scott's back and clasped her arms around his neck, flinging her legs backwards as he stood up into a spin.

The audience gasped again. Someone clapped. Others joined in over the drumbeats and the scratch and cut sounds of the hip-hop music, keeping time with the beat, loving the unusual tunes.

And now Laura and Scott were whizzing across the ice, keeping a clean line, going for the highest levels of difficulty on a double throw loop and then a triple.

Perfect so far. Laura's confidence rose. Scott was totally into the music, skating beautifully. He danced like nothing else in the world mattered, as if he were alone on the local rink and he was just doing his thing.

And so Laura did too, flinging herself into more twists and combination spins, grooving to the sound of the drums that thumped their urgent beat across the arena.

They danced their funky hip-hop dance until the music ended.

There was a second of stunned silence, which seemed to last forever, and then the crowd broke into thunderous applause. People rose to their feet and stamped, lifting their hands over their heads and clapping. The UK fans waved banners and flags. The whole place jumped with the thrill of what they'd just witnessed.

Laura beamed at the excited crowd. Scott looked at her and laughed. "Wicked!"

Together they left the ice.

Vera greeted them with a broad smile. "So perfect!" she told them with tears in her eyes. "Laura, Scott – I could not have asked for more!"

Her coach's praise and tears meant everything to Laura. She flung her arms around her. "Thank you for believing in us!" she said.

Scott too was choked with emotion. "Man, that was the best time!" he sighed.

But now they had to wait for the judges. While the crowd kept up their cheers and chants, Laura, Scott and Vera raised their eyes to the scoreboard.

The scores came up on the electronic board. None of the judges had given a minus score. Three of the nine gave +2 for technical merit, two had awarded top marks for interpretation.

Laura saw the figures dance and blur in front of her eyes. Her mind refused to do the maths. Had they pulled ahead of the Americans, the Russians and the Italians? Had they won gold?

There was a roar from the crowd. Everyone went wild. Other competitors ran up to congratulate them.

"What did we win?" Laura gasped.

"Gold!" Scott said, raising her hand into the air. "We did it, Laura. We won the gold medal!"

For days Laura's feet didn't touch the ground and the smile didn't leave her lips.

There were congratulations and parties, interviews with the press and more parties. Laura and Scott's performance made it onto the sports pages of the Canadian dailies. *Hip Hopping into the Future of Ice Dance! New Kids on the Block Snatch Gold!*

Then they were on the plane home, flying out of Montreal, back to reality. Back to Immy, waiting with Laura's dad at the airport, and big hugs from her kid sister who insisted on wearing Laura's shiny gold medal round her neck as they drove home.

And home, where the parties started all over again with family and friends, where questions rained down on Scott and Laura's heads – "How did it feel to win gold?"

"Were you a bag of nerves?" "Was the hard work worth it?"

In the end, Laura was bored with being a celeb. All she longed to do was get back on the ice and skate.

"I've had it up to here with partying!" she told Scott after their local newspaper had come to the rink to take pictures of them holding up their gold medals and grinning at the camera. "Give me twizzles and death spirals any day!"

He laughed. "I always said you were crazy."

"You mean you're not dying to learn another routine with me?" Laura asked with a grin. She knew full well what Scott's answer would be.

In the distance, Scott's mates were hanging out in the foyer, dressed in United strip, carrying sports bags. They were waiting for Scott to join them for a coaching session at the main training ground.

He made shock-horror gestures and backed away. "No, please, no more Scary

Lady forcing my body into unnatural positions and making me ache from head to toe! No more early mornings, no more bling!"

It was Laura's turn to laugh. "Wimp! But, admit it, you had fun!"

Scott looked her in the eye. "Okay, I did. And you know what?"

"What?"

"You're quite something, Laura Lee. One in a million, if you ask me."

"You too, Scott Yorke," she managed to say. Then there were blushes all round. *Oops, this is getting too serious — let me out of here!* Laura was sad to see Scott go, but excited by the thought of being back on the ice with Vera, training for the next competition, when Patrick's leg would be mended and the old partnership would be in action.

Soon Scott was on his way to meet his mates, hands in pockets, new shades hiding his eyes.

And Laura was on the ice. She was lost in her own world of double lutzes, triple loops and double twists.

Want to read more exciting sports stories? Here's the first chapter from Donna King's latest novel, **Slam Dunk!**

Ashlee ran, weaved and jumped. She flipped the ball into the hoop from the 3-point line.

Tribeca Saints 31, SoHo Panthers 28 in the NYC Community League.

"Go, Saints! Go, Saints!" the fans yelled.

Five minutes to go to the end of the game and the Saints were edging ahead. But the Panthers had the ball; they were dribbling up the court – Ashlee fell back to defend.

"Yeah, Ashlee!" the Saints fans cried as she stole the ball back. She dribbled smoothly past half-court, faked in one direction to give herself an open space to drive to the basket, then pivoted and passed as a Panthers defender closed in.

Marissa caught the ball, faked and passed back to Ashlee. This time Ashlee squared up to the hoop, tucked her elbows in and shot.

The ball kissed off the backboard and dropped through the net.

The referee signalled for two points – 33 to 28. The crowd went wild.

But Ashlee didn't notice them. She saw only the ball and her fellow teammates dressed in their brilliant blue uniforms – tall, lithe girls with long legs and arms that propelled them up to reach the hoop and tip the ball in. She heard only the voice of their coach, Erika Schrader, yelling instructions from the bench.

"Press!" Erika cried as the Panthers inbounded the ball.

The ref quickly blew her whistle, signalling that Marissa had fouled the Panthers' guard. Ashlee sprinted down the court and lined up for the foul shot. The

Panthers' guard shot the free throw off the front end of the rim, and Ashlee leapt up to grab the rebound. The Saints pushed the ball up the floor.

"Great defending!" the crowd roared.

For close on forty minutes they'd watched Ashlee Carson scoop, push, shoot and block the basketball. They'd seen her dribble circles round the Panthers team, twist her torso in mid-air and float the ball through that magical hoop.

Overhead, the rows of lights had dazzled. Out on the court the SoHo Panthers had been left floundering, flat-footed and frustrated.

"How does Ashlee do that?" the crowd cried in astonishment. "Honest to God, I swear I saw that girl fly!"

"Ashlee, where were you?" Theresa Carson was waiting grim-faced for her daughter at the door of their apartment. "I expected you home early tonight."

"The Saints had a game," Ashlee muttered. She flung her schoolbag down in the hallway and headed for the refrigerator.

"How come you never told me?"

"I did."

"I don't remember." Frowning, Theresa searched on the narrow hall table for her keys. "Listen, I'm late for work. I'm going to trust you to do your homework, then get to bed early. You look beat."

"'Hey, Ashlee, how did the game go? Did you win?'" Ashlee mimicked the voice of a sweet, supportive mom, the kind that wore lipstick and baked apple pie. The kind that didn't exist.

Theresa raised her eyebrows. She found her keys. "If I'm late again, I lose my job. If I lose my job, I don't buy your uniform for Queensbridge."

Ashlee frowned and shook her head. She said nothing.

"Do your homework," her mom

repeated, banging the door behind her as she left.

"Footwork fundamentals." Erika began Saturday's coaching session with the basics. She was focused on the four new kids who had joined the Tribeca Saints. "You stand with your weight forward on the balls of your feet, knees bent, hands at five and ten o'clock, butt down. Marissa, you show them."

Ashlee's best friend went into the familiar crouch while Ashlee sat tapping her foot on the sideline. In her head she ran through the new offensive formation that she wanted to practise with the rest of the team.

"From there you can slide left or right or shuffle backwards and forwards," Erika went on. "Simple," she grinned as Marissa demonstrated.

"Hey, Ashlee, where were you after the game last night?" Angelica leaned across the row of leggy girls, all dressed in jogging bottoms and Saints practice jerseys.

"Yeah, Ash, how come you didn't stay behind and celebrate?" Candice asked. "This is the first year ever that we beat the Panthers, and it was mostly down to you."

Ashlee shrugged. "Yeah, sorry. I couldn't make it." She didn't admit that she was at home doing her maths homework, or that her mom was on her case 110 percent of the time.

Ashlee, do your homework. Let me look at your science grade. See how hard I have to work waiting tables at La Sila to buy your uniform. Don't let me down, Ashlee. Work, work, work.

The Queensbridge scholarship exam was in two weeks' time. It loomed ever larger on her mother's horizon – the high peak of the Rocky Mountain range that was their life.

Up and down, up and down went the

Carson family fortunes. Ashlee remembered their life before her dad dumped her mom for a younger, prettier model. She was six years old at the time, the kind of blonde-haired, blue-eyed kid who had it all. There were sunny poolside pictures to prove it.

After her dad vanished for good, Ashlee and her mom had downsized big time. Gone was the luxurious waterside house in Miami. Hello to three rooms in a run-down brownstone in Tribeca – back to Theresa's roots in the old meatpacking district of New York. Rubbish and dirty snowdrifts lining the winter streets, the dash and rattle of the subway trains at the end of their street, the melting-pot school overlooking the wide Hudson where Ashlee first picked up a basketball and discovered she had a real talent.

"Ashlee?" Erika called. "Hey, wake up, girl. Didn't you hear me call the 'A' squad onto the court?"

Starting up from the bench, Ashlee

joined Marissa, Candice, Lindsay and Angelica. Here was action at last, to take her out of herself, to help her forget.

Erika studied Ashlee through narrowed eyes. "That's not like you," she snapped.

"Sorry. What are we doing here?"

"Showing the new kids how to fake," Marissa muttered from the corner of her mouth, handing Ashlee a ball.

"Begin with a head fake," Erika instructed. "Go!"

The five starters gathered at centre court and formed a large circle. They began passing the ball around, faking one way and pressing another.

"That's how you fake a defender – they think you're going to pass to the right, but you pass the opposite way. Lo and behold, you open up some space for a clean pass. Does that make sense?"

The four new kids nodded enthusiastically. They looked up at the starters with admiring glances as they swapped places with them on the floor.

"Ashlee, I want to talk," Erika said, leaving Marissa, Lindsay, Candice and Angelica in charge of coaching the four new recruits. The coach took Ashlee off to the side.

"Are you okay?" she checked.

Ashlee nodded. "Sorry about earlier," she said, blushing. "I had my mind on other things."

"Anything I can help with?"

"No, it's cool."

"Come on, I may look as if I bite, but I promise I won't," Erika urged. She'd been coaching for fifteen years − drilling, teaching them the drop step, the jump shot, the 'give and go'. She prided herself on being able to read a kid's personality as well as anyone.

"No, really." When it came to personal stuff, Ashlee always did this. She shut up tight as a clam. Or she said everything was cool. She faked it off the court as well as on.

Erika sat Ashlee down on the bench. "Okay, so let's take a long, cool look at things. First, I want to tell you how happy I was with your performance last night at point. I was impressed with your leadership qualities – your ability to read the game and motivate the other players. I'd like you to keep that position for the rest of the season."

"Wow!" Ashlee took a deep breath as her roller-coaster life took a sudden upturn. *Hold on tight!*

"Yeah, wow! But seriously, Ashlee, I have high hopes for you."

"Thanks, Erika. I love playing point guard and I won't let you down."

The coach's steel-grey eyes looked deep into Ashlee's blue ones. "You're good enough to make it to the top in women's basketball," she confided. "I mean it, kid, you're heading for the heights – for the junior regional teams and then the nationals, if you want it enough."

Ashlee gave her head a quick shake as she tried to take it all in, then nodded. "I want it!"

"Enough?" Erika double-checked.

"I love playing basketball!" Ashlee insisted. "I live it, breathe it, sleep it. It's all I ever want to do!"

"And nothing's going to stop you?" Erika asked.

At that moment Ashlee felt like one of the subway trains rattling headlong down the track, hurtling through the stations to its final destination. "Nothing," she promised. "When I'm out there on that court, I want to win, believe me!"